The author would like to thank Dr Gerald Legg of the
Booth Museum of Natural History, Brighton, for his help and advice.

VIKING

Published by the Penguin Group
Penguin Books Ltd, 27 Wrights Lane, London W8 5TZ, England
Penguin Putnam Inc., 375 Hudson Street, New York, New York 10014, USA
Penguin Books Australia Ltd, Ringwood, Victoria, Australia
Penguin Books Canada Ltd, 10 Alcorn Avenue, Toronto, Ontario, Canada M4V 3B2
Penguin Books (NZ) Ltd, Cnr Rosedale and Airborne Roads, Albany, Auckland, New Zealand

Penguin Books Ltd, Registered Offices: Harmondsworth, Middlesex, England

First published 1999
1 3 5 7 9 10 8 6 4 2

Text copyright © Theresa Radcliffe, 1999
Illustrations copyright © John Butler, 1999

The moral right of the author and illustrator has been asserted

Manufactured in China by Imago Publishing

British Library Cataloguing in Publication Data
A CIP catalogue record for this book is available from the British Library

ISBN 0-670-87894-4

THERESA RADCLIFFE

Maya, Tiger Cub

Illustrated by
JOHN BUTLER

VIKING

The early morning mist drifted over the Indian forest. In a small clearing by some rocks, two tiger cubs were playing. Little Maya had just grabbed her brother's tail, when a soft growl from their mother called them back to the safety of their den.

It was time for Reshmi, the tigress, to leave her cubs. She was thirsty and needed to find water. The cubs watched her walk quickly away. They knew they must not follow her. They were not the only ones to see Reshmi leave. Beyond the trees, a young hyena crouched and waited.

All night the hyena had kept watch, waiting for a chance to snatch the remains of the deer he had seen Reshmi hide under some leaves. Safe behind the rocks, Maya and her brother, Sameer, had now fallen asleep. They didn't see the hyena creep forwards. He ate nervously, eyes and ears twitching in case the tigress should return.

But Reshmi was already far away, hurrying through the forest towards the lake. High in the trees a peacock caught sight of the tigress and screeched a warning. A group of monkeys took up the cry, their call echoing through the still morning.

Reshmi reached the lake at sunrise. A small herd of deer were feeding on the water plants. They scattered in panic. Reshmi crouched down and began to drink. She lapped hurriedly, anxious to get back to her cubs.

Back in the den, Maya and Sameer had woken. They were hungry and wished Reshmi would return. Maya caught sight of a small lizard and pounced. The creature ran away between the rocks and the little cub followed it, not knowing of the danger lurking outside.

The hyena had just finished the scraps of deer. He loped slowly towards the rocks, sniffing the ground for more remains. He heard a sound, a slight movement. He moved closer.

Little Maya popped up suddenly from behind the rocks. There in front of her was the hyena! For a second she froze, terrified. Then she snarled in fury, baring her teeth, spitting and hissing at the terrible intruder.

The hyena paused, unsure whether to seize the cub or back away. A newborn tiger cub was one thing, this spitting ball of fur and claws was different.

At that moment a great roar filled the forest and suddenly Reshmi was there, leaping towards them. The hyena screamed and fled.

Little Maya was trembling, but her mother was quickly beside her, licking her face to comfort her. Her brave cub had kept the hyena away.

eshmi stayed with the cubs all that day, resting and sleeping in the shade of the rocks. She knew now that it was time for her restless cubs to leave the den. She would take them with her to the lake. She would hide them near her in the long grass while she drank or hunted the deer who came there.

As night fell, Reshmi led Maya and Sameer through the forest. The peacock saw the tigress and screeched his warning once more. Little Maya did not look up. She hurried on, keeping close to her mother and brother. The tigress led her cubs silently into the darkness.